Hey Diddle Diddle

Hey Diddle Diddle

Classic Nursery Rhymes Retold

Joe Rhatigan

Illustrated by Alejandro O'Kif

MoonDance

The little dog laughed to see such sport, and the dish ran away with the spoon.

Hey doodle doodle, the fish and the noodle, tried to climb up a tree.

The elephant danced on the highest branch and said, "Look out below, it's me!"

Hey ladle ladle,
the giraffe in a cradle,
cried for some soup and cheese.

A large sippy cup told him to hush,

and then launched

into space with a sneeze.

Hey clunky clunky, the movie star monkey, went for a ride in his wagon.

While the hot dogs raced to the restaurant,

where they were helped by a kindly dragon.

Hey dapple dapple, the worm in the apple, was hungry for something new.

He moved into a loaf of bread, which he found very hard to chew.

Hey bocker bocker,
the gators played soccer,
but the ball was much too big.

The unicorn mice all clapped and cheered,
while they jumped rope
with the lamp and the pig.

Hey bama bama, two kids and a llama, played catch with some cherry pie.

Quarto is the authority on a wide range of topics.
Quarto educates, entertains, and enriches the lives of our readers—
enthusiasts and lovers of hands-on living.
www.quartoknows.com

MoonDance

6 Orchard Road, Suite 100
Lake Forest, CA 92630
quartoknows.com
Visit our blogs at quartoknows.com

Printed in China
1 3 5 7 9 10 8 6 4 2

MIX
Paper from
responsible sources
FSC® C101537